AKI AND THE FOX

AKIKO HAYASHI

DOUBLEDAY

NEW YORK   LONDON   TORONTO   SYDNEY   AUCKLAND

Kon the fox was bored. He was waiting for the baby to be born. Grandma had sent him all the way from her village near the seashore to watch over the new baby.

Slowly Kon drifted off to sleep. He was dreaming of Grandma's village and the great sand dunes.

When he woke up, a music box was playing softly. There was a tiny bundle in the cradle. Kon felt his heart beat faster—the baby had finally come! She was a beautiful little girl, and her name was Aki.

It didn't bother Kon when Aki chewed on his paws.

When she began to crawl, Aki sometimes squashed Kon. But the little fox never complained.

Soon Aki learned to walk. She often took Kon with her, dragging him by his tail.

Kon didn't mind. He loved playing with Aki. They were always together.

But while Aki grew bigger and bigger, the little fox grew old.

One day Kon's arm burst open. Aki was worried.

"I'm fine, I'm fine," Kon told her calmly. "I'll go back to Grandma's village. She'll know what to do."

"I'll go with you," said Aki. And she hurried to get ready for the journey.

When they arrived at the train station, Kon
walked straight to the platform.

"This is our train. Follow me, Aki," he
said.

The train started to move before they could
sit down. Kon led the way to their seats.

"You take the window seat," said Kon.
"We can watch the countryside, and before
you know it we'll be in Grandma's village."

But Aki remembered that she hadn't
packed anything for lunch. "What if we get
hungry?" she asked.

"Don't worry," Kon answered. "They
sell delicious lunches at the next station."

When the train stopped, Kon jumped
down quickly.

"You wait right here," he told Aki.
"Don't worry, I'll be just fine. The train
won't leave for five minutes." And off he
ran.

Kon got into line, but a lot of people were ahead of him. The line was moving very slowly. "Only two more minutes before the train leaves," he thought anxiously.

Aki waited and waited, but there was no
sign of Kon.

Suddenly the train started with a jolt.
"Kon!" called Aki. But there was no answer,
and she began to cry. The conductor came
by to find out what was wrong.

"If it's a fox you're looking for," he said,
"I just saw one over by the door."

There was Kon, holding their lunches in his paws. When he saw Aki's face he said, "Don't worry, Aki. Our lunches are still warm."

He had jumped back on the train just in time. But his tail was stuck.

"I'm fine, I'm fine," he said cheerfully.
"Go ahead and sit down and we can eat
right here."

"What are you two doing here?"
demanded the startled conductor.

"Don't worry, we have our tickets," Kon
explained. "It's just that my tail is stuck."

The door finally opened at the next stop.
But Kon's beautiful tail was bent in
the middle. The conductor got out his
first-aid kit and bandaged the poor fox
up.

Kon and Aki decided to stay in their seats
for the rest of the trip. Soon they saw the
sea through the window.

They had reached Grandma's village at last.

"Could we take a walk on the sand dunes?"
asked Aki. "I've never seen any before."

Kon looked around. "Grandma's house
is the other way," he said. "But I guess we
could take a quick look."

The dunes stretched as far as they could see.

The two friends were making footprints in
the sand when Aki noticed that someone
had been there before them.

"Whose tracks are these, Kon?" she
asked.

"I don't know," he answered. "Let's find out."

Suddenly they were face to face with a huge
dog. He sniffed Kon's feet.

"Don't be afraid, Aki, I'm here," said
Kon bravely. But before he could say
another word—

Snap! The huge dog picked Kon up and
bounded off toward the top of a dune.

Aki climbed after them as quickly as she could.

From the top of the dune, she could see the
sea and hear the waves. The dog had
disappeared.

"Kon!" shouted Aki. "Kon, where are
you?" But all she heard was the crash of the
waves. Aki kept searching until she found
the dog's footprints around a little pile of
sand.

Quickly she began to dig, and soon
uncovered an ear. She dug faster and
faster, until the little fox was
finally free.

Aki held Kon gently in her arms. His legs
were dangling limply from his body. "Are
you all right?" she asked softly.

"I'm fine, I'm fine," Kon murmured in a
tiny voice.

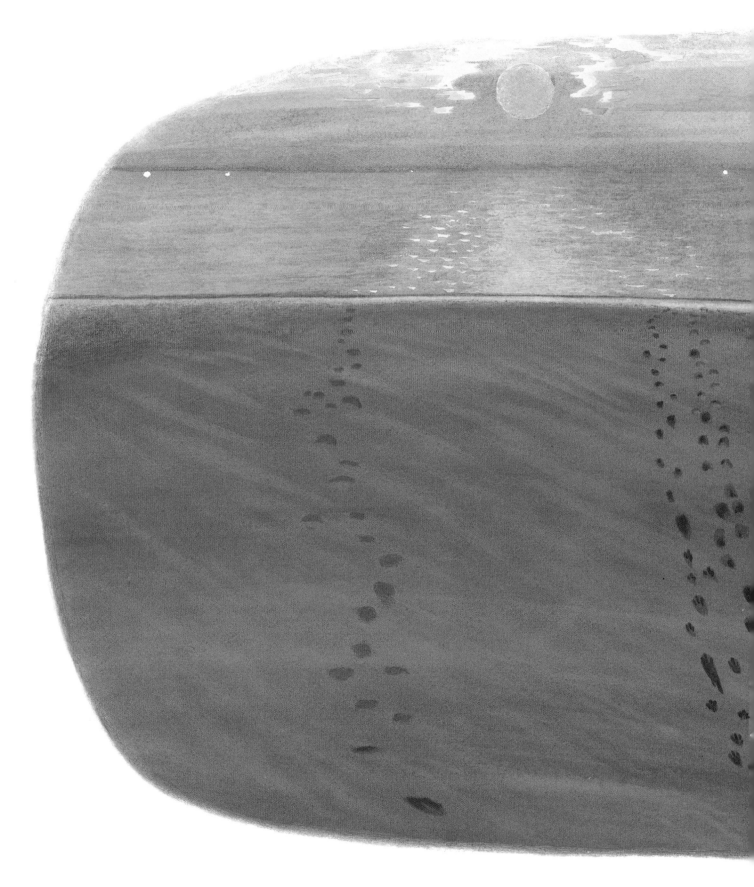

Aki climbed down the dune carrying Kon on her back.

"Which way is Grandma's house?" she asked.
"I'm fine, I'm fine," murmured Kon in the
same tiny voice.

It was getting darker and darker as Aki
hurried toward the houses. There, at the
end of the road, she saw Grandma waiting
for her.

"Hurry, Grandma, hurry," cried Aki. "You
have to help Kon!"

Grandma took Kon in one arm and held
Aki in the other. "It's all right now, Aki,"
she said. "Let's go into the house. But
what's happened to Kon? You two must
have had quite an adventure!"

Grandma went right to work, sewing very
carefully. "He's almost ready," she told
Aki. "All that's left is his tail. And the very
best thing for a bent tail is a hot bath."

When he heard the word "bath". . .

Kon jumped down from Grandma's lap and began to run. "A bath? No way!" he shouted.

But Grandma caught Kon and plunged
him into the clean, hot water.

"Mmmmmmm. This feels wonderful,"
said Aki.

"Well, Kon, a bath isn't so bad after all,
is it?" asked Grandma, smiling.

"It's better than being buried in the
sand," Kon answered.

When Kon got out of the bathtub he dried
off with a big, soft towel. His beautiful tail
was as fat as ever. Thanks to Aki and
Grandma, he looked like a brand-new fox.

The two travelers rested at Grandma's
house, and when the morning came they
were ready to begin the journey home.

PUBLISHED BY DOUBLEDAY
a division of Bantam Doubleday Dell Publishing Group, Inc.
666 Fifth Avenue, New York, New York 10103

DOUBLEDAY
and the portrayal of an anchor with a dolphin
are trademarks of Doubleday, a division of
Bantam Doubleday Dell Publishing Group, Inc.

Library of Congress Cataloging-in-Publication Data
Hayashi, Akiko, 1945–
[Kon and Aki. English]
Aki and the fox / Akiko Hayashi.—1st ed.
p.   cm
Translation of: Kon and Aki.
Summary: Aki and her toy fox Kon make an adventurous journey to
Grandma's house so that she can mend Kon's arm.
[1. Foxes—Fiction. 2. Toys—Fiction. 3. Grandmothers—Fiction.]
I. Title.
PZ7.H3138739Ak 1991
[E]—dc20   90-21577   CIP   AC
ISBN 0-385-41947-3 : —ISBN 0-385-41948-1 (lib. bdg.)
R.L. 2.3
Copyright © 1989 by Akiko Hayashi

ORIGINALLY PUBLISHED BY FUKUINKAN SHOTEN, TOKYO 1989
ALL RIGHTS RESERVED
PRINTED IN JAPAN
OCTOBER 1991
FIRST EDITION IN THE UNITED STATES OF AMERICA